A Foxcub Named Freedom

His new-found freedom could never replace the presence of his mother; he still longed to be near her once again, and even though he would never understand why she no longer wanted him near, he would always love her. Indeed, his dreams were often troubled by fearful images of her being chased across a barren landscape, with no cover, no place to hide. What could it be that pursued her so relentlessly? In his young fox's blood, he knew it to be something terrible . . .

For Christine J.

A Foxcub Named Freedom

Brenda Jobling

First Edition for the United States published 1998
by Barron's Educational Series, Inc.

First published in England by Scholastic Ltd, 1995.

ISBN 0-7641-0600-7

All inquiries should be addressed to:
Barron's Educational Series, Inc.
250 Wireless Boulevard
Hauppauge, New York 11788
http://www.barronseduc.com.

Library of Congress Catalog Card No. 97-49355

Library of Congress Cataloging-in-Publication Data

Jobling, Brenda.
A foxcub named Freedom / Brenda Jobling. — 1st U.S. ed.
p. cm. — (Barron's animal tales)
Summary: A fox cub named Freedom must struggle for survival after his mother is injured.
ISBN 0-7641-0600-7
1. Foxes—Juvenile fiction. [1. Foxes—Fiction.] I. Title.
II. Series.
PZ10.3.J555Fo 1998 97-49355
CIP
AC

PRINTED IN THE UNITED STATES OF AMERICA
9 8 7 6 5 4 3 2 1

Dog fox: adult male fox

Vixen: adult female fox

Brush: a fox's tail

Earth: fox's dwelling, a foxhole

PART 1

Chapter 1

In the undergrowth a vixen lay as still as night; as still as the night that only animals know. For in their world, where whiskers twitch like radar, noses sniff the ground for the scent of prey, and ears are forever tuned to pick up the slightest sound, very little remains perfectly still. Silent, motionless, but alert and watchful.

She lay there watching the sky slip out of its dark nightclothes into a pale blue morning, pink-tinged at the edges. In attempting a slight movement, a sharp pain ran along one of her hind legs and she knew that it would be impossible to stand, let alone stagger home again. Thoughts of her family back in their warm earth tormented her. The cubs, one male and two females, were growing fast, and she was proud of them. Since their father had gone she had loved them even more, trying to make up for his absence by giving them more of her attention. She suspected he had died the death the fox feared most: at the teeth of excited dogs, close to the hooves of panting horses and the sound of human voices urging the hounds on.

Would her cubs have enough skills to help them survive if she never made it back to them? Had they paid attention to those vital lessons she had tried to teach them?

For several weeks the foxes had felt the ground vibrate to the rhythm of galloping hooves and had heard the shriek of birds as they took to the air, startled by the alien sound of the hunting horn. The foxes' keen senses could detect with distaste the sweat of horses, men, and hounds—an acrid stench drifting on the air. The season of the hunt was upon them again and no fox could afford to be caught off guard.

The pain in the vixen's leg had increased so much that she began to feel dizzy, and the early morning sun, although still weak, made her thirsty. She ran her long pink tongue around her lips and sniffed the air. She thought she could distinguish the scent of something familiar. She tried to move again, but once more, searing pain from two gashes in one of her hind legs prevented the least movement. The wounds had been inflicted by some rusty barbed wire, concealed in a hedge she had squeezed through while out searching for food. Maybe she would try again later to move the painful leg.

A spider had begun to spin a web across the bushes in front of her. The fox watched the thin trail of silky cord catching the light, as the dexterous creature wove her beautiful lair. Soon the sun had risen and warmed the damp earth, and the spider was well on her way to completing her task. Suddenly the fox moved her head swiftly to one side, turning her ears toward sounds of movement. Undergrowth crackled beneath the weight of another creature nearby. She lowered her beautiful head, but raised her eyes to see the spider's web vibrate with disturbance in the bushes. In an instant, the leaves parted to reveal another animal.

A pale-coated foxcub moved cautiously toward her. The sight of him made the vixen's heart leap. It was her son. He sniffed her all over, and made gentle nudging movements around her injured hind leg. She tried to move again, to raise herself, but failed. Her actions made him afraid, so he whined and nuzzled close to her for comfort. They lay together for what seemed like ages to the little cub. He loved the smell of his mother, of the

warm, damp fur that kept him and his sisters snug and aware of her as darkness fell. She had never been far from them. At night, watching them as they played on old fallen tree trunks, she had always remained vigilant and responsive to the slightest sound. If ever they strayed too far, she would retrieve them within minutes. Or, if they fell in mud, struggling to rise on all fours again, she would be there too, to fetch them and gently lick the soft fur clean once more.

The little cub knew that he must try to help his mother back to their earth, because that was where he wanted her to be again, close to him and his sisters. But now there was a very real danger at hand. Soon the bright daylight would bring men onto the fields—to work, to walk, and even to hunt.

The little foxcub stood up and tugged at his mother's fur, trying to pull her in the direction of their home, but she could only react by whimpering with pain. He looked at her legs and saw how badly swollen one had become around the big cuts made by the rusty wire. She tried to be brave and looked into her son's soft, round eyes in an attempt to signal that he should go. But he snuggled down at her side again, breathing in her familiar smell, once again drawing comfort from it.

They must have dozed off together for some time, because when they were awakened by a flight of starlings taking to the air, the sun was high in the sky. In her sleep the vixen had dreamed herself back with her cubs and mate, before he had disappeared. The cubs had gamboled before them, and as she studied the differences in their characters, she had tried to find names for them. One vixen she called Frisky because of her lively nature, while the other vixen she named Shy One. This little creature, who always tagged along a few paces behind the others, was gentle and possessed the softest of brown eyes. And then there was the young male who lay curled up next to her now, seeking the protection she knew she would be unable to give if danger threatened. In her dream, she had been trying to find the right name for him. When the starlings woke her, she still had not found a suitable one.

The poor injured vixen felt more than ever the hopelessness of her situation when her ears picked up the sound of approaching humans and her keen sense of smell began to agree with her ears. She woke her small son by nudging him with her nose, using her long snout to prod and urge him up onto his little legs. He was drowsy and chose instead to snuggle even closer to his mother. The humans were now very close so she took stronger measures to make him go, nipping him lightly with her sharp teeth, so that he yelped and staggered to his feet. He looked at his mother, unable to understand her actions. When he tried to resume his position next to her, she drew her teeth back over her gums and snarled menacingly. Then she turned her head away from him, raising it only once more to snarl even more fiercely as he darted to her side. Eventually, bewildered and crestfallen, the rejected cub loped off through the trees.

Her heart was heavy with love for him, and the actions she felt forced to take to protect him hurt her more than the wounds that throbbed in her legs; but this was the only way she felt able to save him, and possibly the other two cubs back in the earth. As he shuffled through the undergrowth, the little cub turned once more to look at her. His last sight of his mother was of her lying curled with her head low to the ground. He whimpered, but she displayed no interest. Tail low, confused, upset, he slowly traced his way back home. His mother watched his retreat and realized that the name for him which had eluded her in her dream was

Freedom. The name was all she could give to him now, and he would never know her parting gift. The fate of Frisky, Shy One, and Freedom was no longer hers to decide.

Chapter 2

Little Freedom eventually found his way back to the earth. As he entered, his sisters, curled up together, woke from their slumber. Their mother's scent was strong on their brother, so they naturally expected to see her too, but she did not appear. The two little vixens searched his face for an explanation, with no response from Freedom other than weary gestures that told them nothing. But soon the sleep of the very young overtook their tired and hungry bodies, and they curled up together for comfort.

Strong pangs of hunger woke Freedom in the evening. His immediate instinct was to turn to his mother, but then he remembered his last sight of her as she had tried to push him away. He felt confused and wondered when he would see her again. He looked at his tiny sleeping sisters, and instinctively knew that he would need to be the provider for the little family group until they were all able to find food and protect themselves.

The air in the young foxes' earth had cooled. Freedom stirred his sisters Frisky and Shy One into wakefulness. Then, in a little procession led by him, they made their way up and out of the short passage to the world above. Freedom cautiously sniffed the air and looked about him. Birds were flying home to their nests, and small creatures such as voles and mice were shifting beneath the woodland floor.

The two sisters started to stretch their wobbly limbs and gently and playfully began

to nudge one another. Soon their playfulness turned into an energetic game of chase, as they ran in and out of the hollow remains of an old tree log. They jumped and rolled over and over, gathering leaves and twigs to their soft fur. They nipped at each other's tails and chased and chewed their own tails.

Freedom would have loved to join in their game but chose instead to keep a vigilant watch over the sisters. Suddenly he froze. Senses keenly sharpened even at their tender age, the other two foxes also became still, aware of possible danger closing in. In near perfect silence, Freedom led his little tribe back to the comparative safety of their earth. One by one they slid down the passageway and curled up tightly together, tired and hungry after their excursion above ground.

All too soon the sound of footsteps and the smell of dogs told them that intruders were near the entrance of the earth. They heard deep voices, and the ground vibrated with the movement of feet above them. A dog whimpered with excitement as he poked his wet, snuffling nose down the entrance to their home. Freedom drew his lips back over the tiny teeth he would have dearly loved to sink into the dog's nose. Up above them, he could hear men's voices laughing, while down below, he could almost hear the hearts of his sisters beating. Then, quite suddenly, the dog's snout was dragged backward, and the footsteps moved away.

Freedom was relieved that his parents had constructed such a fine fortress for their family. It gave him confidence, and he turned to look at his sisters to reassure them that all would be well. The voices, the footsteps, and the damp, meaty smell of the dog soon passed, fading away into the distance.

Before long his sisters dozed off to sleep, like babies exhausted after a short burst of excited play. But Freedom remained vigilant, still listening, just as he had seen his mother do so often. He felt the need to eat gnawing at his small tummy, and the need to feed the two other lives that depended upon him now.

Carefully creeping from the tunnel out into the chilly night air, he sniffed and savored the earthy smells. Stealthily he crossed an open patch of ground in the woods, where the moonlight shone almost as bright as daylight, and made for a clump of trees. Once there, he lay low with his head between his paws, motionless. Within seconds he had pounced high off the ground, landing with a vole firmly secured between his paws and needle-sharp teeth. The creature writhed, then stopped moving.

On his way back to their earth an owl screeched above little Freedom's head, sweeping heavy-bodied through the trees. Freedom paused in his tracks for an instant; then, satisfied that the owl had been disturbed by nothing more than a desire to spread its wings, he continued with his trophy back to the earth.

As he entered the tunnel to his home, the appetizing scent of the freshly killed vole woke his sisters. They devoured the offering greedily. Freedom made several return visits to his sisters, bringing them other small delicacies. Once he almost caught a rabbit, but it proved too quick for him and he missed it by a paw's length. As it bounded off, the rabbit turned its head to look at the little foxcub, as if amazed that something so feeble should have attempted to stalk it.

Tired at last from a night's hunting, and satisfied that the tummies of Frisky and Shy One were full, Freedom settled down to a meal of some furry, stringy remains, all that was left of the sisters' banquet. His stomach was still aching with hunger pangs when he finished the last tasteless scrap of his meal, but the little foxcub was too exhausted to go out hunting once more. As his eyes closed, he vowed that he would soon teach his sisters to hunt and fend for themselves—not too soon, for secretly he had enjoyed the responsibility he had taken for the motherless family.

His new-found freedom could never replace the presence of his mother; he still longed to be near her once again, and even though he would never understand why she no longer wanted him near, he would always love her. Indeed, his dreams were often troubled by fearful images of her being chased across a barren landscape, with no cover, no place to hide. What could it be that pursued her so relentlessly? In his young fox's blood, he knew it to be something terrible.

Chapter 3

Many days passed while Freedom and his sisters Frisky and Shy One learned to hunt and feed themselves from the plentiful supply of small creatures in the woods. Despite the lack of parents to teach them how to survive, the little fox family was existing very well, as each one grew bigger and stronger. They had exchanged their young, fluffy fur for dark, rusty colored coats that lay flat to their sleek bodies. The rounded little noses had lengthened too and their features sharpened, removing the last traces of any resemblance to a foxcub. Fine whiskers grew longer and even more keenly aware of surroundings. Eyes, although still softly colored, now moved with a swift foxy alertness.

When Frisky and Shy One had first started to search out food, they had been lazy in their efforts but, encouraged by Freedom, who had decided to fetch food only for himself in an attempt to spur them on, the little vixens soon proved fearless in their pursuit of small woodland creatures. Occasionally, on a bright, clear morning, the sounds of hunters on horseback would drift downward into their small, warm home. They didn't know that the sound of the huntsmen's horn splitting the woodland peace could be a warning bell for many of their kind; but some inbred instinct as old as the hunt itself told them to beware of that sound.

The little fox family gained more skills to help them survive. All three cubs had mastered the art of belly crawling without disturbing as much as a leaf—very necessary when stalking prey. Freedom seemed especially good at it. He would lie camouflaged amongst bracken, barely breathing, until a small rodent almost walked into his mouth. Or, if he felt that the creature he was stalking had become aware of him, he would pause while it looked about, then he would slither like a snake until he was nearer, and suddenly leap into the air with a perfectly arched back, before securing the prey between his paws.

Even in the early days of the little family's forays into the world above ground, they had sensed that in their territory they were the hunters, the creatures from which other animals fled. Rabbits, mice, ducks, chickens—all lived in fear of the cunning fox. As they set out for food to devour, or to stock up their larder for another day, each one of them knew their strengths: a sharp sense of smell, perfect hearing, a body built for speed, and a clever, cunning brain. But they were still young and had yet to realize that the squeeze of a trigger, the blast from a hunting horn, or the screech of brakes could signal death for them.

As Freedom and his sisters grew more and more to resemble young foxes, they began to travel further afield. They became more adventurous too. Once Frisky, led by her overly inquisitive nature, had strolled far from her own territory and found herself close to a railway embankment.

Frisky listened, fascinated by the strange hum the rails were making. But what had really caught her attention was the sight of a small, brown, furry vole, scurrying along the other side of the railway track. She tiptoed over the first railway line and was just about to step over the other rail and pounce, when she realized to her horror that the end of her tail had become trapped beneath a railroad tie.

Frisky twisted, turned, tugged and pulled

at the tail until all her muscles ached with the effort. Terrified and exhausted, the poor young vixen rested for a moment, but only to discover that the rails were now giving out a much louder humming sound, as well as a tingling sensation which ran up her tail, making her whole body shake. Looking up in terror, she saw in the distance the bullet-shaped nose of an enormous train, tearing along the track toward her.

Once again the vixen began to tug at her tail, stretching every sinew in the effort to free it, but still it stuck fast. The train was almost upon her—death was imminent. Then, as she felt heat from the great beast bearing down upon her, she tried one last maneuver. With her tail still wedged, she threw her body over the side of the rail and down the embankment. Before she could gather her senses, the train had roared past, leaving behind only twigs and leaves twirling in the air.

Frisky stood up, still dazed. All her shaking limbs were in place! Although her muscles hurt from the effort of struggling, she could see no dreadful cuts, just a few scratches. Then, as she gazed up at the track, she received a shock that hit her with almost as much impact as the sight of the train. Blowing in the breeze between the rails was the end of her tail—her precious tail. It had saved her life, but at what price? She had received admiring glances from all the foxes in her territory ever since it had started to grow soft and bushy and very, very long.

The poor vixen licked at the place where the ginger fur and her tail had parted company. There was still lots of tail left, but to Frisky, it would never seem the same again.

In the future, Frisky stayed well away from the railway lines, except to watch from a safe distance as the trains raced by. She knew in those moments that the tip of her tail had been a small price to pay after all.

It wasn't only Frisky who came close to death. Shy One once found herself unable to free a small chicken bone which had become lodged in her throat. She had snatched the bird from a chicken run, squeezing through a weak spot in the fence. The three foxes had dined well on the plump flesh and licked their whiskers at the end of the meal, so as not to miss any of the delicious taste. All the remaining bones lay on the ground except for one little sliver, no thicker than a needle, that had become wedged across Shy One's throat. She coughed repeatedly in an attempt to free it, but it remained stuck.

By nightfall she had found it increasingly hard to breathe. Frisky and Freedom listened to her dreadful wheezing, and took it in turns to fetch water in their mouths, which they trickled onto her head and into her mouth to cool her.

By the end of the next day, when the sun had turned the color of the leaves from gold to deep pink and birds were winging their way home, Shy One suddenly stood up on wavering legs. She looked as though she was about to draw her last breath and Freedom and Frisky were afraid. But instead of collapsing and dying, she produced four massive coughs, which shook her body so violently that the last one brought with it a small puddle of water, in the middle of which floated the soggy remains of the chicken bone!

An hour in the cool evening air and lots of water to drink put Shy One on the way to recovery. It was at least a week before she could eat anything, and Freedom and Frisky had to chew her food first to make it soft enough for her to swallow. But even when she was eventually well enough to hunt and feed properly again, her brother and sister always watched her out of the corner of their eyes when chicken was for dinner.

Out exploring, Freedom came across some old farm buildings, surrounded by high black railings. Although his acute sense of hearing and smell informed him that no humans were about, his nostrils twitched as he moved nearer and saw a duck pond crowded with sleepy ducks. Peering left and right, while keeping his body low to the ground, young Freedom crossed the clearing to the railings. Carefully squeezing between a gap in the bars, he padded lightly over to a rusty hay barn, where an ancient tractor stood rotted into the ground. It was near the ducks who, so far, hadn't suspected his presence.

As Freedom moved closer to the pond, he sensed movement some way off, approaching at high speed. He looked about for somewhere to hide and headed back to the barn. Carefully, he lowered himself down into the long grass to one side. Snuggling low, he made himself hardly visible. Within minutes a van thundered through the gates, which crashed shut behind the vehicle as it screeched to a halt in a cloud of dust. The doors burst open, spilling out two ugly-looking dogs and two even uglier men. The men were shabbily dressed and unshaven. Their dogs looked extremely ferocious as they barked with excitement when the smell of Freedom reached their nostrils.

"Be quiet, Jason!" shouted the taller of the two men to his dog. "Otherwise there'll be no dinner for you."

But the dog continued to bark despite his master's warning.

Then the other dog joined in. His master responded by shouting, "What's the matter with you? Something's up for sure. I reckon they've got the scent of an animal," he suggested. "Maybe we'll get a nice juicy bunny for the pot tonight."

The men laughed as they encouraged the dogs to go off and follow the scent that interested them so much.

"Go on, Champ! Fetch us back a nice big bunny rabbit," one of them bellowed.

Freedom could see the dogs from his hiding place and he wondered whether he should stay put or make a dash for it. But as the fearsome creatures neared, baring their teeth and drooling from the corners of their mouths, the fox left his cover and headed off toward the farm buildings. This proved to be a bad move. Far better the territory he knew than the unknown.

As Freedom dashed between the farm buildings, looking for shelter or a way out, he thought he could feel the hot breath of the dogs warming his tail. He could see no immediate way out and raced wildly about the yard, scattering the ducks. Now there was another danger to be faced: when the two men spotted him, they seized the opportunity for what they imagined to be a bit of fun. From the back of the van they produced loaded rifles which they fired near the fox as he ran, aiming to terrify rather than kill him —that would be left to their dogs.

Exhaustion overtook Freedom as he circled the yard again and saw the barn and old tractor coming into view. An idea slipped into his mind. It was a very lean chance, but anything was worth trying! If he could reach the railings again and squeeze through, the dogs would be too big to follow. He would need to slow them down just long enough to permit him time to wriggle between the bars. He had to try it, although if he became stuck, the dogs would kill him.

With a plan in mind, Freedom was able to summon up a final reserve of strength. Looking toward the men, he rushed straight at them with amazing speed. They saw him coming and started to roar with laughter at the brave fox's attack.

"Here, foxy, foxy!" the big one called, choking with laughter. "I'll just get my little gun ready for you. Seeing as how you're so kind as to come looking for me, I'd hate to disappoint you!"

But as the men hurriedly attempted to reload, Freedom made a valiant dash straight at them, running swiftly between their legs. The dogs, still close on his tail, followed and tried to copy him, but they were too big and their weight knocked their owners over like bowling pins.

This was just what Freedom had hoped for—enough time to make his escape. As he dashed toward the railings and squeezed through the narrow bars, he looked back for a second to see the tangle of dogs and angry men attempting to free themselves.

Once clear of the railings, Freedom ran on, his breath burning in his throat and his muscles drained of energy. When he reached the trees, he slowed to a gentle trot homeward, until the sound of the dogs' barking could barely be heard above his panting.

Chapter 4

As the months went by the three foxes began to grow more independent of one another. Often, prompted by the desire to show herself to dog foxes in search of a mate, Frisky would parade her beauty, responding readily to their calls. Her coat shone and her brush swept the ground as she moved slinkily and provocatively between the trees. When she found a mate, it would be for life, so she had good reason to be choosy. Frisky was courted by several ardent males, some of whom had traveled a long way, before settling in her new earth with a handsome, gentle mate.

Eventually, even Shy One left the security of home life. Her partner had endured a long courtship before she finally moved off with him, but his persistence had paid off and they were to share many happy years.

With his sisters comfortably settled, Freedom at last felt able to listen to the call within himself to search out a mate.

Now, whenever he moved through the woodlands or across the fields at night, he was strongly aware of the scent of young vixens. He would listen for their calls and screeches, so exciting to a young dog fox, especially when seeking a partner.

One evening, as the sky darkened and the air became filled with scuttlings, squeakings, snufflings, and barks that were audible only to animals of the night, Freedom followed close on the trail of a vixen. He could hear her enticing calls and in response he opened his mouth, and from deep within his throat uttered a cry that told the vixen he was near.

In a patch of moonlight that shone brightly through the trees stood a sleek young vixen, her fine features enhanced by the pale blue glow of the moon. She was an impressive sight. When Freedom saw her, he knew straightaway that his search had ended—but first he had to court her. He needed to show her that, above all others, she was the most desirable.

Slowly he edged his way toward her. She turned her head to face him and blinked. Freedom felt encouraged, so he moved a few paces nearer. This time she responded by moving toward him. Then, when they were close enough, they sniffed one another and walked around each other in circles. Freedom smelled good to the young vixen, and he thought that she gave off the most wonderful aroma he had ever experienced.

The two foxes continued to circle one another, stopping now and then to break into little games of chase, just like the ones Freedom had enjoyed as a cub with his sisters. Then they sniffed one another again, and gave playful nips and tugs. Through these games they were discovering whether they were suited for each other, and it didn't take Freedom and the beautiful vixen long to find out how well they were matched.

Freedom joined the vixen in the earth she had prepared. It was warm and clean with lots of room to stretch out or curl up together. In the spring she would give birth to their cubs, and the months Freedom had spent in rearing himself and his sisters would be of great value to them all.

Freedom and his mate lived happily and comfortably in their earth with its passages and cozy chambers. The vixen was a good hunter, sharp-eyed with incredibly quick reflexes. Freedom felt proud when he watched her in action, as she moved with speed and amazing accuracy.

When the weather had warmed enough to coax the first spring flowers out of the ground, Freedom's mate gave birth to their cubs: two males and one female. Their mother licked their tiny bodies clean and fed them her precious milk before falling into an exhausted sleep. Freedom was thrilled at the sight of his new family, and while they slept, he set about tracking down tasty morsels for his mate to eat.

Throughout the first week of the cubs' life, Freedom continued to provide his mate with all her food. One night, after a long search, he realized that he lacked success because he was so tired and hungry himself. His catch for the night had been one tiny mouse. As he entered the earth with the little offering dangling from his jaws, he noticed how quiet it seemed. For a moment he panicked—until he reached the bottom of the passage and caught sight of

his mate and her babies curled up fast asleep. Silently he devoured the meal, looking on with pleasure at his family. The tiny heads of the cubs were barely visible above their mother's long brush, wrapped around them for warmth.

Freedom and his mate made excellent parents, always watchful and forever attentive to the cubs' needs. When they had grown enough to venture outside, Freedom led them up to their first sight of the world above. It was late in the evening and the cubs staggered and wobbled about wherever their father decided to go. Soon his mate joined them. As soon as the little cubs caught her scent, they left their father and wobbled over to their mother, nuzzling into her side for protection and warmth.

Freedom settled into his new role as a responsible parent, careful to keep his family within reach. He found most of their needs for nourishment in his locality, but at times it was necessary to travel farther afield. On those occasions he sometimes found plentiful supplies, which he buried in a trench for later use.

It was while Freedom was out on the longer journeys that he would sometimes catch sight of his sisters. It made him feel proud to remember how he had helped raise them. They had been transformed into beautiful vixens with their own families.

One evening as he padded his way through the trees, he caught a glimpse of his sister Frisky. She still moved gracefully and her coat gleamed with a healthy sheen. Her mate and her cubs were near her, so Freedom remained at a distance.

Frisky fussed over her cubs, which amused Freedom, until he realized that one of them was holding a vicious snake between his teeth. The little cub enjoyed the way the snake wriggled and writhed, but he was unaware that one bite could prove fatal. Freedom stayed hidden behind a thick tree trunk, but prepared himself to spring from his cover and seize the snake at the right moment. To his amazement, he suddenly saw his sister leap into the air and land right on top of her cub, who was so taken by surprise that he dropped the snake immediately, watching as it slithered away beneath the carpet of leaves. Freedom moved away silently, feeling proud of his sister. She had grown up to be a match for any woodland creature.

Chapter 5

As the weeks went by, Freedom's young cubs became very active. It was difficult to keep them from scampering off up the passage as soon as they sensed the evening had arrived. They couldn't wait to follow their parents out of the earth, rushing off, each cub pursuing a different direction. Freedom found himself constantly retrieving them.

The mock battles they loved to play seemed rough to their mother, but only occasionally was one of them injured. Once, one of the males whimpered over to her, rubbing a blood-soaked ear with his paw. She licked it clean and fussed over him for a few moments before watching him bound away, rejoining the same fighting game that had just caused the injury.

The cubs grew at a steady rate and it wasn't long before Freedom proudly led them out on nightly hunting parties. He soon found that all three of them were quick to learn the skills he had acquired when young. He watched how keen they were to spring into action and enjoyed seeing them make the same mistakes he had made as a very young fox, like leaping after a leaf because the wind had stirred it so that it resembled a small creature. Freedom taught them to smell first—and leap after!

On some nights though, the cubs didn't want to hunt or practice listening to the signals other foxes and animals put out. They were only interested in playing. Sometimes their games of chase took them too far away, but Freedom was usually quick to find them again.

One evening, the little fox family left their earth to stretch their limbs in the cool air and find food. The moment the cubs' inquisitive little noses inhaled the sweet evening air they became excited, and what started out as a game of chase rapidly developed into hide and seek. Their mother was very tired, as the cubs had slept restlessly throughout the day. Selecting a spot at the base of an old stump, she stationed herself there to watch over her children. Freedom padded around the cubs as they played, his sharp senses focused on food to feed his family. The cubs' game took them farther afield and several times Freedom retrieved them, but they were cunning and scampered off again.

It was while Freedom was catching his breath, pausing a few moments before concentrating on some serious hunting, that he noticed the two males crawling low to the ground. It pleased him to see them trying out a hunting technique he had shown them. Just then, the little vixen trotted over to him. Freedom looked down at her and blinked affectionately.

He returned from his thoughts and looked up to watch his sons, but to his surprise, they were nowhere to be seen. He looked all around—they seemed to have disappeared. For a moment he felt panic rising, but he stopped and reasoned with himself; the cubs

couldn't have gone very far—could they?

He checked the undergrowth, near to where they were crawling, but there was no sign of them there. He sniffed the air for their scent but it was everywhere they had played. He called, in the hope that they would hear him and follow his calls back home. He extended the area of his search for paw prints, scent, or anything to point him in the right direction. His keen sense of hearing turned his head from side to side, in the hope of

picking up their excited yelps and growls—but without success.

His mate and daughter were distressed to see Freedom return without the cubs. He led them back down into the earth and shared a light meal of the remains of some small animal. Then he watched his mate curl up with their daughter and look sadly back at him as he moved off up the passageway to resume the search for their precious missing cubs.

Outside the earth, the evening had turned into night. The scent of other animals was sharp in Freedom's nostrils. He could smell the sort of creatures he loved to hunt, but tonight he wasn't interested—he was on the trail of his sons.

The fox trudged on through woodland, his ears tuned to pick up both near and distant sounds and his eyes darting toward the slightest movement. He remembered how easy it had been when he was a cub to wander off from the earth, traveling a long way at times. As he continued to pad along, his mind became plagued by visions of accidents that could have befallen the cubs: they could have fallen down a bank and lie injured, or one could even be caught in a trap! His thoughts continued to torture him as he journeyed onward.

After several hours of searching, Freedom stopped. He needed to rest. The sky was a deep, velvety blue and stars twinkled brightly overhead. Looking about, he saw a hollow tree trunk. He crawled into it. As his fur brushed against the inside, bits of bark and insects fell onto his coat, but he was too tired to notice. Just before he fell asleep, he thought of his mate and their little daughter, safe and warm inside their home. His daughter would be fast asleep, but he knew his mate would be awake, and alert, listening and sniffing for scents that would tell her of the return of Freedom and the precious cubs.

Chapter 6

Freedom slept well that night, with his thick brush wrapped around his legs and head to keep him warm, despite being woken up twice. The first time he heard a badger foraging close to his shelter while its young ones played and tumbled nearby. The second time the scent of foxes and cubs aroused his sharp sense of smell and he sniffed at the air with his wet, pointed nose, but the scent did not belong to his cubs.

When he fell asleep after the second disturbance, he slept until the warmth of the morning sun shone onto the tip of his nose and forced him to open his eyes. He was drowsy. Above him, the birds spoke to one another in their own beautiful language of song. But it was the raucous cawing of rooks and the irritable chattering of magpies that filled Freedom's ears and, like an alarm call, shook him into wakefulness. Up! It was time to be on the move.

Emerging from the tree trunk, he shook himself and gave his whiskers a quick lick. He sniffed the air but could not detect the faintest whisper of the cubs' scent. Looking around to see which direction he had come from the night before, he noticed a path ahead, passing through the bushes and trees. He decided to follow it. Whether it went round in circles or just disappeared into brambles like so many woodland paths, it would at least be leading somewhere.

Freedom had not thought to feed himself on his journey, and despite the grumbling noises that his stomach made, he felt he could not swallow anything until his mission had been accomplished. As he padded along, the sun shone down through the trees, raising his spirits. Deep down, however, he knew that the day might end without sight of the precious cubs.

He trotted onward to where the path broadened. There he saw old and new footprints of many kinds of animals. He sensed that the track led somewhere special to them, like a stream or an open field, plentiful in insects, rodents, and grass.

Following the track, he eventually found an area where the trees began to thin out. The path had widened even more and bore the hoofprints of horses and footprints of humans. This worried Freedom. Although the prints were not fresh, they told him that the track was well used by both. In the distance he could see the trees thinning out even more, where they met the edge of a field.

With renewed vigor, he broke into a faster trot toward the field.

As the fox drew nearer to the field, he passed by a bush and for some reason felt impelled to stop there. Despite the urgency of his mission, the feeling that he had been there before was so strong that he knew it must hold some special meaning for him. He stood very still, compelling himself to work out why the place had affected him. What could it be?

He let his eyes wander slowly over the bush and scenery around him. He couldn't remember ever having been there in his life, yet the strange sensation persisted. He was about to put it to the back of his mind and concentrate on the more important quest for his sons, when a flood of memories and emotions rekindled the pain and loss from deep within him.

Quite by chance, he had found the place where he had last seen his mother many months ago. He wandered over to the bush and lay down in the spot where she had collapsed, badly injured. He looked around. What had he expected to see? His mother, healed and waiting for him? As he lay there, trying to conjure up her face, her scent, and her warmth, he remembered only confusion and rejection—she had pushed him away that day.

Suddenly Freedom was shocked back into reality by sounds that warned him to be on guard. Far off in the distance, the voices of people drifted toward him. Stealthily, he crept to the edge of the big field, which ran upward and had high hedges reaching across it. He peered through the long grass, looking in the direction of the sounds. In the distance he could make out a group of young boys carrying sticks, which they used to whack carelessly at the grasses and flowers.

Freedom's first reaction was to slip back into the undergrowth and head for a deeper part of the woods. There he would find a place to hide until the potential danger had passed. Just as he was about to turn away, he became aware of movement in the long grass farther up the field, and in the air he caught a faint but unmistakable scent. He raised his wet, sensitive nose to the sky, and sniffed sharply. There it was again!

Deep in the long grass, and totally unaware of their father's—or anyone else's—presence, two foxcubs romped, nipping at one another's tails playfully, wrestling, and growling. As soon as Freedom set eyes on his sons, he wanted to rush straight over to them, but because the boys were getting nearer by the second, he didn't want to attract them—the cubs would be so excited to see him. He had to move them, and quick! Freedom felt he would do anything to save his children, even at the sacrifice of his own life.

Checking his position, he saw that he was about halfway between the boys and the cubs.

Flattening himself to the ground, he crawled toward his playful sons. As he moved, he could feel vibrations in the ground as the boys advanced, and he heard the swish of their sticks through the grass. Within seconds they would hear or see the cubs.

When he was only a couple of body lengths away from his cubs, who had begun to act even more excitedly as their father's scent reached their wet little noses, Freedom heard one of the boys shout, "Hey! What's that in the grass over there?"

It was the only signal Freedom needed. Swiftly, he slithered toward the little cubs and, grabbing the startled creatures in his mouth by the loose fur at the back of their necks, he hurled them, one at a time, into the bushes. Then, before they had a chance to realize what was happening, the fox dragged them back into the undergrowth, covering them with his sleek body. The cubs were so afraid at the speed with which they had been whisked away from their games, that they stayed silent.

Within minutes the boys had reached the bushes near to where Freedom lay protecting his sons. He could hear the swish of their sticks again as they disturbed the brambles and leaves above them. One of the boys poked his stick only a whisker away from Freedom's nose.

"I reckon it must be a cat you saw," he suggested.

"Or a rabbit—there's loads of them around here," offered another one of the group. "Anyway, whatever it was, it's gone now. Come on. Let's get out of here!"

When he was sure the boys had gone, Freedom rolled himself away from the cubs and lay licking their sweaty fur into shape. They responded with affection. How could he be angry with them? They were so young and had no idea how dangerous the world could be.

After a brief rest, Freedom started to trot homeward, keeping the hungry and exhausted little cubs a few paces ahead of him. As he passed the place he had paused at earlier, he understood the reasons for his mother's actions that day. Just as he had protected his sons, and would have given his life for them, so had his mother saved him in much the same way. It was clear to him now that she had shielded him from the possibility of harm by shooing him away. It had been all

she could do, injured and incapable as she was of any other defense of her cub. For so long it had felt like rejection; now, as an adult with cubs of his own, he was at last able to understand. Whatever her fate had been, he would never forget her bravery.

Freedom returned home with the cubs, who were greeted eagerly by his mate and daughter. From then on, they were soon brought back into line by a sharp nip from their parents if they strayed too far outside the earth.

As the little cubs grew rapidly into young foxes, the males took a keen interest in the call of young vixens. The need to find a mate could take them far away, but they were good hunters, and if no rabbits or small animals were available, then fruit would suffice.

One evening, when only one of his cubs had still not found a mate, Freedom rose and went up the tunnel to breathe the cool night air. Suddenly he heard a young vixen in the distance. Her calls were barely discernible, but he hadn't been the only member of his family to hear them—through the trees, he glimpsed the outline of his son.

Freedom wanted to go after him—just pad along the trail for a little way—but he knew that his son must travel alone on this journey to find a partner for life.

He returned to the earth, which seemed so spacious again now that his sons and daughter had departed, and looked at his mate curled up asleep. She had been a good mother to the cubs. As he drifted off into a deep sleep, thoughts of his own mother came into his mind.

PART 2

Chapter 7

Freedom was never to discover the fate that had awaited his mother when, as a cub, he had stumbled his way back to his sisters.

The vixen lay low in the undergrowth after he had gone, the scent of humans and a dog increasing as they moved nearer to her. And with the scent had come sounds: first the voices of a girl and an elderly woman, then the deeper tones of an old man's voice beckoning to the dog. Enticed by the scent of the wounded vixen, the old labrador ignored the calls of his master and plodded his way toward the bushes where the fox lay helpless.

The vixen caught sight of the dog before he was able to focus upon her with his old, cataract-glazed eyes. Instinct told her to lower herself as deeply as possible in the grass, but the dog's wet, prying nose found her all the same. She snarled and he barked, a repeatedly throaty bark, thrusting his doddering old head at her as he opened a wet and foul-smelling mouth.

It didn't take the people long to reach him. The girl was first.

"What have you found, Jas? Another rotten old ball?" she teased. She peered more closely into the grass, then drew in a sharp breath and pulled the dog away, motioning to her grandparents to proceed quietly.

The old man and woman advanced with caution toward the injured vixen, the woman recoiling a little when she saw the gashes in the creature's hind leg. By now, the girl had sunk to her knees in front of the wounded animal.

"Oh, you poor, poor thing!" she cried. "We've got to help her, Grandad—she's in an awful mess."

The swelling around the cuts, and the congealing blood which had matted flesh and fur together, looked horrible. When the old man had finished calming the dog and had tied him to a tree, he too went back for a closer inspection of the injured vixen.

He saw immediately that infection had set into the wounds and knew that death from such wounds could be slow and painful. He advised his wife and granddaughter to go on ahead with the old labrador, despite the girl's protests, then took off his heavy raincoat and wrapped it carefully around the vixen. At first she snapped at him, then whimpered with the pain of her efforts. Once he had lifted her into his arms and begun to take slow and measured steps with her held firmly in his arms, she relaxed a little and resigned herself to the fact that he did not appear to mean her any harm.

Slowly they made their way to a whitewashed cottage about two fields away, situated at the end of a long, rough track. While his wife led the old labrador into a kennel in the yard, the old man carried the vixen into the kitchen and placed her on a large wooden table in the center of the room. His granddaughter followed close on his heels.

Trying not to cause the vixen any added pain, he felt the wounded leg to see if it was broken as well as badly cut. But the gashes were so red and swollen that the creature flinched at the slightest touch. Next, he examined her to see if there were any other cuts, noticing as he did that the fox was an adult vixen, who could well have cubs back in her earth. He stroked her head. She felt very hot, and he knew this was probably due to infection in the wounds.

“This isn’t going to be easy, Anna,” the old man told his granddaughter, “but I must try to clean this poor vixen’s wounds and make her comfortable. I don’t hold out much hope for her—she looks too weak to survive.”

Anna’s eyes began to fill with tears but she tried to be brave and held her head up. Her grandmother put an arm around the girl’s shoulder and whispered to her, “We’ll do our best for her, dear.”

Anna smiled and said, “Perhaps the vet will come out and have a look at her.” Her grandfather, Robert, agreed that it would be a good idea, but he wanted to clean her up and make her comfortable first.

Without further delay, Robert fetched a bowl of warm water and disinfectant. Then Mary, his wife, restrained the fox while her husband cleaned away the congealed blood and earth from around the gashes. It caused the vixen pain, and she struggled feebly as the warm liquid made contact with her open wounds, but she made no attempt to bite the old people. Making a skillful team, they cooed to the vixen until the damaged area was cleansed of dirt and blood. Then they laid her carefully in an old log basket, which Anna had been busily lining with warm blankets, and put it by the hearth.

Mary offered the vixen water, and although she moved her mouth toward it, she did not drink, but rested her beautiful head on the edge of the basket and fell into an exhausted sleep. Anna stood looking thoughtfully at the pathetic creature for some time, wondering if she would ever wake again.

Robert telephoned James Winton, the local vet who had cared for their labrador since his early days as a playful puppy, and left a message on his answering machine, asking him to visit. Jas was barking loudly, confused by being left outside rather than allowed indoors to his basket. As Robert returned to the kitchen, his wife glanced up at him and, motioning with her eyes for him to look at the fox, whispered, "She's so weak, Robert."

Once the fox had been placed in the big basket, Anna wouldn't leave her side. The old couple joined her, kneeling next to their granddaughter in the warmth of their cottage kitchen, which had sheltered many wild animals over the years. When their own four children had been young, they had brought all sorts of injured creatures home—birds with broken wings, field mice who had survived cat attacks, and even a slow worm with the tip of its tail missing had been carried in lovingly by small hands—but never a fox, until that day. Most of the animals had been nursed back to health and released. Others, less fortunate, had breathed their last in the little kitchen and been buried later under the apple tree.

The ticking of the clock had a comforting sound, Anna thought. She loved to be with her grandparents. Life in the little cottage

seemed to her to be "real" living, right next to nature. Where else would she, such a devoted animal lover, ever see a fox in a kitchen? True, she didn't live far away, but the view from her bedroom window at home looked out onto neatly fenced gardens, not wild fields, birds, and . . . foxes! Her grandparents didn't need a garden—the whole of the countryside was there for them. She was twelve now, and for as long as she could remember, she had always loved her visits. This time she was staying for a whole month during the summer vacation while her mother and father were away on business.

A sudden knocking at the kitchen door startled Anna. Robert stood up and let James Winton in. Striding into the kitchen, the tall, middle-aged man smiled as he spoke.

"I got your call, Robert, and came straight away," he said. "Now, where's this poor creature that's causing you concern? I thought your days of taking in injured wild animals had stopped when your children grew up! You'd probably have put me, and my father before me, out of business if those animals had been livestock or pets."

The vet smiled at Robert and Mary and they chuckled at his praise. Robert led him over to the vixen and the vet knelt down and studied her wounds carefully. Anna placed herself right next to him, making it difficult for him to move freely.

"Don't worry, young lady," the vet assured her, "I'm not going to hurt her." Anna took a step backwards and smiled at the vet. Then, just as Robert had done, he too checked to see if the leg was broken, and ran a hand over her head and looked into her eyes.

"You've made a lovely job of cleaning this nasty wound. Judging by the look of her, she's tangled with some sharp wire fairly recently," he said, continuing his examination. "And, although I'm pretty certain that her leg isn't broken, the cuts are long and badly infected."

From his bag he produced a syringe and a small vial of pale yellow liquid. Anna looked concerned.

"I'm going to give her an injection of antibiotics to help clear the infection. I'll give you some for her in tablet form too. Try to get it down her throughout the week. If she survives the next forty-eight hours, she'll probably recover, but she'll need a lot of care and attention to build up her strength again. I don't need to tell you how exhausting looking after injured wild animals can be."

Robert held the vixen still while James inserted the needle into the loose flesh around her neck. Anna made herself look. She would need to be ready to help in the days to come, so it did little good to flinch at the sight of messy wounds or a needle.

"There you are, my beauty. Just lie back now and let these good people give you their special care. You couldn't be in better hands." He smiled as he closed his bag. The vixen hadn't struggled this time—she was too weak. Soon she was sleeping.

Chapter 8

Late that night while Anna and her grandparents slept soundly, despite the rumblings of a distant storm, the vixen awoke. The odors of the kitchen were unfamiliar to her nostrils. She tried to move but her legs felt heavy and extremely painful. She lay motionless in the dim light provided by the moon, able to distinguish the peculiar shapes of objects without knowing their function. Cupboards, chairs, pots and pans were all around. Some made peculiar sounds, like the ticking clock and the dripping tap.

Her head swam with the strangeness of it all, but for some reason she didn't feel in any immediate danger.

As the vixen lay there, thoughts of her cubs suddenly flooded into her mind. She tried to push the thoughts away, but failed. They faded only when she was disturbed by the sound of footsteps on the stairs. She lowered her head down into the basket. There was nowhere for her to hide, as the footsteps drew nearer . . .

In the dim light, Anna glided across the tiled floor of the kitchen toward the fox. Feeling her way around, she knelt down beside the basket and strained her eyes to see the outline of the creature.

"Just checking that you're all right, poor fox," the girl whispered.

The vixen heard her speak, but remained with her head buried low. Anna continued, "I know how weak you feel now, but soon you'll feel a lot better."

She moved closer but didn't touch the animal, breathing in a mixture of the disinfectant used to clean the wounds and a grassy, meaty smell that was the fox's own odor. The vixen's instinct was to snarl, but for some inexplicable reason she refrained and stayed silent and still, as though hypnotized by the girl who hovered above her.

A sudden movement nearby made Anna catch her breath. The vixen had sensed it first but didn't move a whisker. Fox and girl were locked together in a bond of silence. Someone else was in the room! Anna could hear breathing close by, and it was moving closer . . .

The kitchen light flashed on just as the storm which had been approaching announced its arrival with a resounding clap of thunder. The illuminated room looked like a scene from an old silent film. Clenching a raised walking stick in one hand, while the other held the rolled-up newspaper he'd used to knock the light switch on, stood Anna's grandfather, ready to attack an intruder. Opposite him, Anna stood shielding the fox, arms thrust out stiffly from her sides and slippered feet wide apart. Her woolly dressing gown had fallen open to reveal a long T-shirt adorned with boldly printed pictures of hedgehogs, badgers, foxes, and field mice and bearing the highly appropriate slogan, "100% WILD ANIMAL LOVER."

Grandfather and granddaughter stood as still as wax figures, staring wildly at one another.

"Grandad!" shrieked Anna.

"Anna!" retorted her grandfather.

The old man recovered from his shock by gulping down a glass of water, gripping the side of the sink for support. Anna had slumped down into an old armchair. They looked at one another and burst out laughing, clamping their hands to their mouths to stifle the sound, in case it frightened the fox or woke Mary.

"You should have seen yourself, Grandad," chuckled Anna. "If I'd been an intruder, what use would a newspaper have been to you? I suppose you were going to read him into submission!" she spluttered.

"That's enough! I certainly scared you, Miss," the old man replied, trying hard not to laugh. Then, shaking his head, he went on, "I just knew you wouldn't be able to stay away from that poor fox for long. I know you're worried about her, but she needs rest and peace if she's to recover. If she survives the next few days, then you can take over looking after her until she's ready to leave us."

The old man smiled as Anna threw her arms around his neck and thanked him. She knew that every word he had spoken made good sense.

"Now, since you're here, you can help me to give her some more of the antibiotics the vet left. I was on my way to do it when I heard an intruder moving about," Robert chuckled.

Anna had always been special to her grandfather. He loved all of his five grandchildren, but Anna was his favorite.

Robert encouraged her to hold the vixen's head gently but firmly, while he coaxed open one side of the animal's mouth. Then, using a teaspoon, he tipped a mixture of ground-up tablet and a little water into the vixen's mouth.

"Good girl! That's the way. You drink it all up for me." Anna's grandfather stroked the vixen's head and gave her some water in the same way that he had administered the medicine.

Only when Anna and her grandfather had gone back to their beds did the vixen open her eyes fully again. She was bewildered by the activity of the past hour, and anxiety about her cubs returned to plague her. Eventually, through sheer exhaustion, she slipped into a deep sleep that was to last almost until lunchtime the next day. During that time, Anna and her grandfather managed to sneak two more doses of the antibiotics into her mouth. They did it so skillfully that she stirred only slightly in her sleep.

Chapter 9

Anna got up early the next morning in the hope of spending extra time with the vixen. Remembering her grandfather's words from the night before, she decided to keep a respectful distance. Her grandparents had been up for an hour already and her grandfather had given Jas his first walk of the day. Jas was in a state of confusion—he didn't understand why the kitchen remained out of bounds to him when it smelled so deliciously of fox.

Anna helped her grandmother to assemble

fresh brown eggs, tender, pink bacon, and crusty bread for breakfast.

"It might be my imagination, Anna, but that fox seems just a little better this morning—not quite so limp-looking, somehow," commented Anna's grandmother. Anna put an arm around her and kissed the top of her fluffy gray curls.

"Still early days, Gran, but I sort of know she'll be all right. Grandad said that I could take care of her all by myself when she starts to improve. Isn't that great?"

"Just so long as it doesn't require you to go creeping around in the night again!" chirped the old lady.

After breakfast, Anna helped her grandfather make repairs to an old outhouse that hadn't stood up very well to the previous winter's storms.

It was while they sat together later, enjoying bowls of rich homemade soup and chunks of bread, that Anna suddenly nudged her grandfather's arm, silently motioning him to look in the direction of the vixen. The creature, having woken from her long sleep, had lifted her head and sniffed at her wounds before licking them. Anna's grandmother had been right—the fox didn't look quite so ill. Although she still appeared to be very weak, there was definitely something about the way she held her head that showed strength returning to her body.

Anna's grandfather continued to administer the antibiotics, with Anna close by his side. On the third evening the vixen attempted to shuffle herself around in her basket, which prompted Anna's grandmother to fetch a larger, stronger one she had been saving to store wood in.

"Let's see if she'll take some food before we move her. I'm afraid it's only going to be some of old Jas's mashed up dog food," Robert whispered to the fox, "but if you can get it down, why, you'll be chasing my old dog around the garden in no time!"

The vixen stuck out her long, whiskered nose toward the pale brown mixture and inhaled its meaty aroma. It certainly didn't smell like freshly killed rabbit or vole. She let her head slump over the edge of the box and shut her eyes in silent protest. No food had passed her lips for several days, but still she preferred to go without, rather than attempt

the dog meat. The choosy vixen liked her food raw.

The three of them maneuvered the vixen into her new, bigger basket, then sat back and watched her as she sniffed around, licked her wounds again, and dozed off.

That night, before going to bed, Mary placed a small plate of raw chicken pieces in front of the vixen's basket.

Chapter 10

Mary was the first downstairs the next morning, eager to see if her tempting chicken morsels had been eaten. She looked at the bowl. It was upturned and empty. Also gone, she realized with a shock that made her stomach turn somersaults, was the fox!

Anna's grandmother made a lightning search of the kitchen, then unlocked the back door and looked outside into the yard, even though she knew there was no way the fox could have escaped through the bolted door. Hurriedly, she clambered upstairs to rouse her husband, trying all the while not to wake Anna, in case the fox had met with a grim end.

The old man was soon dressed and downstairs, making a thorough search of all the rooms.

"I don't understand it—she's just disappeared," his wife kept repeating to herself while she opened cupboard doors and peered inside.

Suddenly, Robert pointed to what looked like several drops of dried blood on the tiled floor, and then noticed a few more leading in the direction of the old butler sink. A curtain was suspended beneath the sink, which Robert very cautiously drew aside. At first glance, all that could be seen were bottles of cleaning fluids and rags, torn up to make dusters. Then, gently moving aside a pile of newspapers, Robert and Mary found themselves staring at what appeared to be a piece torn from an old fur coat, lying limp and discarded beneath the sink pipes. It was the fox.

"It doesn't look good, Mary," said the old man shaking his head. "Let's try to get her out before Anna comes downstairs."

As quietly as possible, they removed all the articles from under the sink. Then Robert crawled into the cramped space toward the fox. Reaching out a shaky old hand he gently felt the vixen's coat. It was warm. By gradually easing her forward, he managed to maneuver her out of the confined space and into the early morning sunlight that was beginning to filter into the kitchen.

A quick but thorough examination showed Robert that the wound had opened up again and bled. The vixen was weak and exhausted from the activity of trying to move about, so he stroked her beautiful rust-colored head to comfort her.

"I reckon she was trying to get up on her legs again, to find her way back to her real home," said Robert. He continued to stroke her head, trying to soothe and reassure her. "But I suppose we should take her efforts as a sign of improvement. At least she's tried."

"And look at this!" His wife smiled, holding out a small plate for her husband's inspection. "She's eaten every scrap of the chicken I put out for her last night."

When Anna arrived in the kitchen she was greeted by the sight of her grandfather dabbing at the fox's wounds to clean them once again, while her grandmother was wiping the spots of blood off the floor.

"Gran! Grandad! What's happened?" the girl cried out in alarm.

"Nothing to be upset about, dear. Our visitor just had a little fall. She decided to go for a walk in our kitchen last night, but it was a bit too much for her stiff legs," replied her grandfather, now drying the wounds.

* * *

Anna devoted the next two days keeping constant watch over the vixen, but without fussing over her. She kept a respectful distance and confined herself to preparing the chicken scraps, and changing any wet or messy bedding.

The vet phoned. He was both surprised and delighted to hear that the fox was still alive and slowly improving. Robert had not lost his touch with wild creatures, and James Winton considered that to be a very special gift.

"She'll need to stretch her legs soon, Robert," advised the vet. "Outside would be the best place for her to exercise. If you can rig up some very basic form of shelter and fencing, it would be a start toward getting her back to her own environment."

The vet's suggestion set the old man thinking. If he cleared out the recently repaired outhouse and erected some wire fencing around it, he could make it comfortable with some fresh straw. Then the vixen would have plenty of room to move and stretch her legs, both inside and outside her new dwelling.

Anna was eager to help when her grandfather told her of his idea. So the next morning, while the vixen slept, they set about the task of moving the contents of the outhouse into an old shed, and driving posts into the ground for wire fencing that would help create an enclosure.

Watching all the strenuous activity from a safe distance, was Jas. Lying flat on the ground with his floppy head between his paws, his face bore a distinct expression of confusion. It was as though he somehow sensed that all this hard work had something to do with the creature in the kitchen who had suddenly come into his life, robbing him of his rightful place by the hearth.

By lunchtime, Anna and her grandfather had almost completed the fencing. All that remained was to make a trip into town to purchase some straw, and the new housing for the fox would be complete. The old car, which was hardly ever used, surprised Robert by roaring into life at the first turn of the ignition key. After a short drive into the town where Anna lived, they returned with several bales of fresh straw on the back seat. The straw smelled sweet to Anna as she scattered it about the interior of the old outhouse, at one end of which her grandfather had set out two large feeding bowls. One was full to the brim with fresh water and the other contained some more scraps of chicken.

It didn't take them long to install the vixen in her new home. Anna's grandfather positioned the bedding at the back of the outhouse, so that if she attempted to walk again in the night, she would at least be sheltered if she fell.

It was dusk when the latch on the new enclosure clicked shut for the day. At first, the vixen had shown little interest in her new surroundings, but by the time Anna and her grandfather had gone indoors and washed their hands, they could hear distinct sounds of movement from inside the vixen's new dwelling. Anna looked out the window as she dried her hands.

"Grandad," she began inquiringly, "do you think I ought to just pop my head around her door and see if she's all right?"

"Definitely not, dear!" the old man answered, smiling. "I think she's probably making herself comfortable—sort of moving in and making it her own."

That night, when most humans were settling down to sleep and most creatures of the night were just beginning to go about the business of their wakeful hours, the vixen stretched out her front legs, opened her long, wide mouth and yawned. With every inward breath she could scent the familiar smells of the countryside about her. Twitching her ears, she could identify the different sounds of creatures nearby: badgers scuttled laboriously on pointed feet, like someone weighed down by heavy shopping bags; mice slid almost noiselessly through the undergrowth; and an owl flapped its wings under the effort of carrying its heavy body to an unfortunate mouse's hiding place. The vixen's keen sense of smell could even detect the scent of other foxes, and not that far away either.

But the odor that interested her most at the moment was coming from the scraps of chicken. Her foxy instincts had been sharpened by her new outdoor surroundings. For the first time in days she felt the urge to hunt for her food—to catch it, feed on it, and draw strength from its goodness. But she knew that her legs would give her little support, let alone carry her swift-footed on the trail of a rabbit or a vole. And of course, there was the tall fence that stood between her and the world she knew.

Using all the power in her front legs, she managed to drag herself a little way toward the chicken. It tasted good. When she had finished eating, she licked her whiskers thoroughly with her long pink tongue. Then, noticing the water bowl, she rapidly lapped up all of its contents.

As she moved back to the heaped straw in the corner, she felt exhausted. Pain returned to the wounds, but she soon fell asleep, worn out by her efforts.

Before the first rooster had crowed his scratchy alarm call the next morning, Anna had risen and dressed. She crept downstairs, taking great care not to rouse Jas, who was sleeping noisily but contentedly once more in his basket in the kitchen. She put on her coat and slipped out the kitchen door.

Outside, all was quiet. Very carefully, Anna tiptoed over to the vixen's living quarters. She peered through the wire fencing and into the outhouse until her eyesight became accustomed to its dark interior, where she focused on the fox. Fast asleep and curled up in the straw, the vixen appeared to have very little wrong with her.

The young girl felt her heart suddenly beat faster. Was it excitement over the improvement the vixen was displaying, or fear that she was recovering and would soon yearn for her freedom?

Chapter 11

As the vixen's health and strength continued to improve, Anna took over more and more of the responsibility of attending to the animal's daily needs. She realized with mixed feelings that her parents would soon be home and the vacation over. It all added up to her being parted from the precious vixen.

Her parents returned, and although Anna was delighted to see them again, they sensed a sadness about her which Robert soon explained. He told them of Anna's complete devotion to the fox and of how she had worked so hard to help the vixen recover. Then he suggested Anna should stay with them until the vixen had fully recovered. After a few minutes of discussion her parents agreed, but only so long as school and homework came first. Anna was ecstatic and promised all sorts of improbable results at school as a reward.

When she returned to school, though, her thoughts were often with the animal she was impatient to get back to at the end of the day. Was the vixen all right? Had she eaten all the meals put out for her? Had she tried to stand, but fallen? Several times a day Anna was reminded by her teachers that her schoolwork was to be found in front of her, and not out the window.

As soon as she got back from school in the afternoon, she would change into her old jeans and boots. Then, grabbing a chunk of her grandmother's fruitcake and cramming as much of it as possible into her mouth, she would head directly for the fox.

She took great care not to frighten or disturb the vixen as she lifted the latch to the compound and stepped carefully over to the outhouse. When she had finished cleaning the living quarters—putting down fresh straw, food, and water—she would gently inspect the fox's wounds to insure that no further infection had set in.

"There now, my friend—it's me again. How are you feeling? Shall we jog a little together today? Perhaps not today then, but soon."

Gently whispering words of reassurance, Anna gained the vixen's trust enough to allow her to examine the wounded area. As she approached, the fox's golden eyes flickered from side to side, taking in the whole scene, possibly poised for flight, even in her condition. She was still very much part of the wild territory she had come from.

Anna's daily devotion to the vixen made her grandparents very proud of her. The fox gradually began to sense that the girl meant her no harm, and showed it by allowing her to move freely about the outhouse and run, without displaying any obvious alarm. The young girl loved the way in which the beautiful animal had begun to trust her. She delighted in seeing the vixen look up whenever she entered the run and, on recognizing her, blink and lower her eyes. Anna felt flattered that the fox showed her this silent gesture of familiarity. Some nights she lay awake wondering about the vixen. Where had she come from? Was she a mother? If so, did her cubs need her?

One evening before bed, Anna took out some scraps for the vixen. As she lifted the latch to enter the run, she suddenly realized that the animal was not in the outhouse. Slowly creeping to the back of the run, she was greeted by a sight that took her breath away. The vixen was standing unsteadily on all four feet. She turned her head toward Anna, blinked in her usual form of greeting, and then, pausing for a few seconds as though making some sort of decision, wobbled forward past the girl and into the outhouse. Anna wanted to jump up and down with excitement; instead, she quietly left the run, tiptoed into the kitchen to her grandparents, and announced excitedly, "Gran! Grandad! You've got to see her—she's walking!"

Chapter 12

James Winton paid a brief unannounced visit to the cottage one afternoon to examine the vixen.

"Well, Robert, you and your wife are still working the old magic by the look of things. The wound has cleared up beautifully—and she's gaining weight. The eyes look good as well," he said, congratulating Robert and Mary.

"Nothing to do with us—it's that young granddaughter of ours. She's devoted to the creature," Robert said proudly.

"Well then, tell her for me that she could make a good vet one day," smiled James. His face took on a more serious expression as he said, "But Robert, I am just a little concerned that the vixen's wounds may have affected the nerves in her hind legs. That could slow her down and make it difficult for her to fend for herself and hunt for food in her natural environment. She still needs time to build up strength in those muscles."

Later that day, Robert passed on the vet's comments and compliments to his granddaughter. Anna was both pleased and flattered, but she was upset to learn of the possible damage to the vixen's hind legs.

The vixen steadily improved, and by the end of the week she could walk with confidence and even trot with style. Anna had watched the animal trying her legs out for the first time in this fashion. The initial attempt had brought the poor creature flat on the ground.

She had looked shocked, but not in pain, and seemed just a little humiliated by her lack of dignity. Undaunted, she had got up again for another go, and that time she had succeeded. Round and round the little compound the vixen had trotted, almost as though she was afraid to stop, in case she couldn't get going again.

One night, there was a terrific storm. Anna knocked on her grandparents' bedroom door and asked if she could bring the animal indoors, but Robert told her not to worry—the fox had probably survived many storms before coming to live with them.

Outside, the lightning lit up the landscape, highlighting the gleam in two foxy eyes that were busily surveying her territory. The rain was heavy and lashed at the fencing and posts. A little work with front paws might unearth weaknesses in the construction—just enough room for a fox to squeeze under. But old Robert had done his job extremely well, sinking the fencing deep into the ground—deep enough to keep even the craftiest vixen safely inside.

Robert had known for a few weeks that the time would soon arrive for the vixen to be set free, although he understood how foolish it would be to let her go before she was really fit.

James Winton continued to visit the cottage from time to time, and with every visit he was delighted to see that the vixen was improving. On one visit, almost a year to the day since she had arrived at the cottage, he pronounced her to be fit and in good, healthy shape once again. All that remained of the wounds were scars, and they would stay hidden beneath her shiny, deep red coat. His only concern was the occasional stiffness she still displayed in her legs. This made her limp if she moved too suddenly, but he could find no trace of the damage he suspected might prevent her from leading a normal life once again. It was time for her to return to the woods and fields, to a way of life she had known before her accident.

Old Robert had sensed the change occurring in the vixen. During the day she would prowl along the edge of the fence. He would talk to her as he had always done, but she never stopped by him or took any tidbits. She knew that there had once been another life out there beyond the fence, and she wanted to be part of it again, no matter what might lie ahead for her. Robert also knew that the hardest part of letting her go would be the sadness it would bring to Anna. What he didn't know was that Anna was already contemplating the noticeable change in the vixen too. Separation was imminent—inevitable. One afternoon, she voiced her thoughts.

"I knew she would need to go one day, Grandad, but are you really sure she's ready to look after herself? Are her legs strong enough to support her in the cold winters?

Will she remember how to hunt?" Anna fired her questions with a frown on her pretty face.

"Anna, I can't give you the answers to all of those questions," the old man replied, "because I don't know them. The only thing I'm certain of is that she should be free."

A day was arranged for the vixen to be released, close to the spot where she had been found. On the appointed day, James Winton arrived. He brought with him a strong metal cage, padded to protect the vixen on the short journey to where old Jas had found her.

Anna spent a long time in the run with the vixen the evening before her release. She wanted to sit in front of the fox and take in every feature, every whisker, so that she would be able to recall the sharp, silent face whenever she chose to in the future. But what could possibly fill the empty space that face would leave behind?

When the time came, Anna stood silently

and bravely by as the vet entered the run. Carefully, he introduced the vixen to the cage. She entered it cautiously, but without fear. Anna, her grandfather, and the vet then drove with the caged vixen to the path leading to the exact spot where she had lain injured among the bushes. Together, Robert and the vet removed the cage from the van and carried it along the path.

Anna fought back tears and tried to smile. She had refused her grandmother's advice to stay home and let the two men release the vixen alone. The vet warned the girl and her grandfather to remain absolutely still as he slowly removed the front of the cage, lifting it a little at a time.

The vixen stood up and sniffed at the air. One paw moved cautiously to the edge of the cage, where she paused and looked about her until her eyes came to rest on Anna. She blinked, then slowly brought the other paw over the edge. There she stood, poised

between two worlds. She raised her lovely head as she sniffed at the air again, as though scenting something familiar. Then—she was gone! A swift trot into the bushes—and gone. Nothing remained except the empty cage to bear witness to a beautiful animal who had become the focus of a family's daily attention for a whole year.

All the way back to the cottage, Anna both laughed and cried, convincing herself that the vixen who had shared her affection for so long was far happier back in her own environment. She had fought hard not to make a pet of the fox, reminding herself on many occasions that she was not going to mold a wild creature into a tame companion, although at times it had been difficult.

Chapter 13

There was little anyone could do to help Anna through the following weeks. She often walked to the bushes where she had last seen the vixen, but never saw her again. Sometimes she fancied that the fox was watching her from the cover of the thicket, but she knew that the animal would be concerned with more immediate needs than looking out for the girl who came from that other world.

Anna knew that it would take a long time to get over the fox's departure. She relived the happy memories of hours spent watching the animal, and treasured a tiny tuft of rust-colored fur found in the bedding the vixen had slept on. Even old Jas, recently restored to his rightful place as the center of attention in the household, couldn't console her. Time and again he dragged his leash to her feet and dropped it, only to retrieve it minutes later and plod off rejected. For a whole year he had been restricted to going in and out of the cottage by the front door only, unless accompanied by Robert. Once he had slipped into the yard unnoticed and suddenly come upon the vixen in her run. She had smelled good to him, but the teeth she bared, and the menacing look in her yellow eyes, had forced him into a cowardly retreat.

Anna returned home and throughout the next month threw herself into her schoolwork in an attempt to forget the pain of losing the fox. One evening, she received an excited phone call from her grandmother. The vet, James Winton, had been so impressed by the way in which the girl had cared for the vixen, that he wanted to know whether she would be interested in helping out at his office over weekends and during school vacation, providing her parents agreed. He thought she would be well suited to comforting pets coming in for treatment and operations. When she reached fourteen he would be able to pay her something, but for the present she must consider it good training for a future vet—should she decide on such a career.

Anna's grandmother took it that the squeals of delight at the other end of the telephone signaled Anna's acceptance of the generous offer.

PART 3

Chapter 14

On the day the vixen was released, Anna had felt a sharp pain of loss for the first time in her life. The vixen's feelings were confused: one moment she was in the run, the next, back where she had longed to be throughout her convalescence. It felt strange to her. For a whole year she had been fed regularly on tasty morsels, but tonight she would need to sharpen up her hunting skills if she was to nourish herself.

She stayed in the bushes just long enough to see Anna, her grandfather, and the vet depart, Anna looking back from time to time. Soon the sound of their voices faded and the girl's familiar figure disappeared.

The vixen stretched out her legs and yawned, looking around her as she did so. The sights and sounds of the wildlife about her flooded her entire being and awakened her senses to their former keenness. Within an hour of her release, she had found her way back to the old earth she once shared with her mate and cubs. There was no sign of life inside. A few bones of small animals, left over from meals, remained, as well as a faint odor of her children—but the scent was somehow richer, more developed, than that of cubs. She returned up the passageway to the daylight, and wondered to herself whether her children still lived, and if so, how far away?

Time passed, and the vixen had made a secure new home for herself. She prowled and hunted competently in the woods at night, but as she aged, she hunted with less vigor. On some mornings, when the frosty grass broke rather than bent beneath her cold paws, she would search the bushes for berries or old fruit to feed herself. Many of the rodents were hibernating, so the foxes would take whatever there was.

When snow carpeted the ground and the streams and ponds were frozen over, the vixen licked at the snow for moisture. As she wandered the woods searching for food, she listened for the familiar sounds of neighboring foxes, ever alert for the ones she had once called her children. On some days she would embark on a long journey in the hope of finding a trace of one of them—but always without success.

Then, one sharply cold morning, with a chill in the air that made her old wounds ache, the vixen heard the sound of a hunting horn. She thought she could also detect a gentle pulsing, a vibration in the ground, such as that made by the movement of many horses and riders. Instead of retreating farther into her earth until the sounds and sensations passed, she felt strangely drawn toward the direction of the noise.

That horn signaled fear for even the bravest of foxes, so why did she feel as though she were being pulled toward it? As she advanced, the sounds became louder and clearer, and the pungent odor of men, dogs, and sweating horses made her feel dizzy; it was the smell of death.

She was now at the edge of the field, and as she padded the last few steps that separated her from the cover of bushes and trees, she suddenly caught a faint whisper of a wonderful scent in the air. It was a scent she knew—the odor of another fox, one to which her own body had given life. It was her son Freedom.

With eyes wide open she watched, rooted to the spot, as Freedom traveled the length of the field. He showed no fear as he ran ahead of the motley pack of humans out to run him to the ground. He ran fast and he ran free. They wouldn't catch him! Then, as her handsome, fully grown son dashed by, and her heart swelled with pride as she watched him change course in order to slow his pursuers while he disappeared under a hedge, she suddenly remembered another fox on another day, making for that very same hedge —a hedge that was reinforced by sharp, rusty barbed wire. At the memory of the cruel barbs tearing into her flesh she winced, realizing with horror that her son was probably about to be caught in exactly the same way. But he would have no time to wriggle and tear himself free as she had done, for the hounds were too close and would soon be upon him. She needed to act quickly.

Summoning every ounce of courage left in her body and directing all her energy to her weakened hind legs, she sprang through the cover of the bushes at the edge of the field and flashed her flaming, chestnut coat at the hunters and their dogs. Then she ran at them, almost head-on, to attract their attention.

"Look at me! Take me!" she seemed to say.

Two of the dogs caught her scent at once, and the leading rider, the first to spot her, signaled her presence to the others, making them aware that it wasn't the same creature they had been so busily pursuing.

Confusion had already broken out among the hounds. Some were breaking away to follow the new, rich scent the vixen trailed as she sped away from the hedge. She ran as she had never run before, in her mind a single thought—to lead them away from her son. When she reached the corner of the field, she doubled back and chased in crazy fashion back across to the other side, intentionally keeping in full view of the hunting party.

The hunt members were by now

completely divided: some jostled around the hedge where young Freedom was last sighted, while others pursued the erratic antics of the vixen as she led them a merry dance, confounding them with her zigzagging maneuvers before finally disappearing into a thicket to one side of the field.

After half an hour of total confusion, the master of the hunt sounded his horn to summon the hounds and riders who followed. He had decided to call off the hunt. It had been a strange day for the hunters, and certainly one that would provide them with a tale to tell for many seasons.

They finally departed, leaving the vixen lying deep in a thicket. She was exhausted. The site of her old injuries had begun to throb with acute pain, and her limbs were rapidly stiffening as hot sweat turned to an icy dampness on her fur. As she listened to the sounds of the hunters retreating, uppermost in her mind was her concern for her son Freedom. She longed for a glimpse of him, to see for herself that he lived.

A strange sensation in the vixen's chest, which had begun as a tight feeling, made her breathing increasingly painful. It wasn't the pain of heartache for a son she feared dead or dying, but the pain of a heart signaling the end of its life. All the months she had spent at the cottage as she healed and became strong again had equipped her for a quieter life in the wild, not one that included the sort of encounter she had just experienced. Anna and her grandparents had nursed her back from near death, but as she had aged, the weakness the wounds had inflicted had begun to show. She was no longer able to recover from prolonged chases.

As the pain came again, and she looked up into the trees to see the brightness of day, she breathed in her last breath, full of the rich earthiness that reminded her of so much she loved.

The vixen was never to see her son again, but as she took her last breath and shook from the sharp spasm of pain around her heart, she fancied that suddenly he also breathed somewhere near to her. She felt his presence, and it was enough.

She had been right. Her son Freedom was nearby when she died. He had survived the hunt, hidden deep in the hedge where even the scent-crazed muzzles of the hounds could not reach him, and had emerged unmarked but for a few scratches from the wire. At the sound of the hunters' departure, he had waited a few minutes before picking his way along the hedge to the edge of the field. There, in the thicket, he found his mother. He stood above her, looking down on her still, warm body, that even in death gave off enough scent to tell him of their relationship.

Freedom recalled the last time he had been close to her. He wanted her to know how proud he felt to be her son, longing for her life to be restored, even for a moment. Now, only one thought emerged to comfort him: she had risked and given her life freely—it had not been taken from her. No pack of humans on horses, or cowards with guns could ever tear it away from her now.

He stood looking at the body until the light faded. Nature would take her body, and her spirit would run free over the landscape, across the fields where there was no cover, only the sky above and the earth below; an earth that belonged to God alone, who in time returned all His creatures to it.